THIS BOOK BELONGS TO

_____

_____

A LITTLE OWL BOOK
A DAY AT THE ZOO

by Hilda Young
illustrated by Susan Aspey

WORLD

Sally and Peter were very excited. Mummy and Daddy were taking them to the zoo to see all the different kinds of animals there.

"Now remember, children, some of these animals are very fierce," warned Daddy. "You must not go too near them."

"We'll be very careful!" promised the twins, as everyone joined to the queue to buy tickets to get into the zoo.

As they passed through the turnstiles, Sally gave a little squeal of excitement.

"Oh, look, you can *ride* on some of the animals!" she cried. "Please may I have a ride on one of the elephants, Mr. Keeper?"

"Certainly," replied the keeper. "Kneel, Rajah!" he ordered.

And to the children's amazement, the large grey elephant knelt down so that Sally could climb onto the seat on his back.

"I feel like a princess!" she cried.

"Let's go and see the big cats now," suggested Daddy.
"You won't be able to ride *them!* They will all be safely
behind bars."

So off they went to admire the lions and tigers.

10

Sally jumped as one lion gave a mighty roar.

"He's only telling us that he's the king of the jungle," Mummy said. "Aren't the little lion cubs pretty?"

"They look just like cousin Janet's marmalade pussy!" chuckled Sally.

In the next cage two proud tigers paced back and
forth, staring at Sally and Peter with their bright golden
eyes. One tiger yawned, showing some very sharp teeth.
"I'm glad I'm not his dentist!" laughed Peter.

"Just look at the panther's black coat!" said Daddy. "It shines like silk. The panther is a type of leopard, children. Look, there's a spotted leopard in the next cage. Isn't he magnificent?"

A large crowd had gathered around the big pool where the polar bears lived.

"It must be feeding time," explained Daddy. "Yes, watch them catch the fish their keeper is throwing to them!"

"Aren't they clever!" cried Peter.

"I'd rather have my fish cooked for lunch!" Sally said.

A little further away a group of monkeys, munching bananas, were watching the chimpanzees holding their own tea party.

The table was set with cups and saucers, a teapot and a plate of sandwiches.

"Peanut butter, I suppose!" said Sally as one of the chimps tried to give her a sandwich.

As they walked on they came to the open-air part of the zoo, where animals were allowed to roam about in their own natural habitat.

A kangaroo came bounding up, almost knocking Peter over, on her way to join a mob of kangaroos in the distance.

"Oh, look, Peter, there's a baby kangaroo sticking his head out of his mother's pouch!" cried Sally.

As they peered over the fence the children saw several zebras and various kinds of antelopes.

"What graceful creatures the gazelles are!" cried Mummy. "And just look at that giraffe, nibbling away at the leaves at the top of those tall trees."

"His long neck is certainly useful," agreed Daddy.

"And his coat is just like a jigsaw puzzle!" cried Peter.

"Goodness, what a loud noise!" cried Peter, as they walked on.

"It's coming from the Bird House," laughed Daddy. "Parrots are very noisy birds. Just listen to them!"

Inside the Bird House as well as all the parrots there were small brightly-coloured humming birds, woodpeckers, mimicking mynah birds and a pair of haughty eagles with strong, powerful claws.

"There are birds here from every part of the world," said Daddy.

As they strolled through the deer park, eating ice-cream, Sally suddenly saw lots of children climbing into a strange object.

"What are they doing, Mummy?" she asked. "It looks just like a giant Noah's Ark."

"It's part of the special Children's Zoo," Mummy explained. "Daddy and I can go in the zoo with you, but only you and Peter can go in the ark."

"Come on, Peter, let's go to the children's zoo!" begged Sally.

Inside, the twins quickly realised that the ark was a very exciting place.

Sally was allowed to hold a fluffy white rabbit, and Peter fed a cheeky chipmunk with grain from a bag that the keeper gave him.

There were lots of mice and hamsters, doves in a dove-cote cooing softly, two chattering cocks and hens, some brightly coloured guinea fowl . . . two in fact of everything small or cuddly or that you could safely feed.

"It really was lovely, Mummy," cried Sally, as they looked around the rest of the children's zoo, admiring the proud peacocks, the sheep with their lambs, the large-horned goat, the ornamental ducks and the tiny darting fish in the pond.

"So you've enjoyed your day out at the zoo, have you?" asked Daddy.

"Oh, yes," replied Sally and Peter together. "Please may we come again soon? There is so much to see and do!"